Milo

and the

Moon
Kangaroo

In memory of Maxine - DT

And a big thank you to Emma Blackburn,
Nia Roberts and Jane Buckley
at Simon and Schuster.

SIMON AND SCHUSTER
First published in Great Britain in 2010
by Simon and Schuster UK Ltd
1st Floor, 222 Gray's Inn Road, London, WC1X 8HB
A CBS Company

Text and illustrations copyright © 2010 Dan Taylor

The right of Dan Taylor to be identified
as the author and illustrator of this work
has been asserted by him in accordance with the Copyright,
Designs and Patents Act, 1988

A CIP catalogue record for this book is available
from the British Library upon request

ISBN: 978-1-84738-328-0 (HB)
ISBN: 978-1-84738-329-7 (PB)

Printed in China

13 5 7 9 10 8 6 4 2

Milo
and the
Moon
Kangaroo

Dan Taylor

SIMON AND SCHUSTER
London · New York · Sydney

It was way past bedtime and an imaginative
Milo Montgomery was busy doodling instead
of sleeping. He was just about to colour in
a dinosaur attacking a skyscraper when . . .

Oh, no!

He noticed that his favourite green crayon was missing.

Milo thought hard about where it could be.
Then he remembered! That afternoon,
he had been using his crayons in the garden.

Milo rushed to his bedroom window
and peered into the garden below.
There, glistening in the moonlight,
was a green crayon trail!
Milo raced downstairs.

He followed the trail along the garden path,

through the garden gate,

down Mortimer Street,

through the park and
straight into . . .

A jungle!

"Have you seen my favourite green crayon?" asked Milo, as he swung through the vines with a bunch of mischievous monkeys.

But nobody had.

So Milo swung higher and higher
right onto . . .

A pirate ship!

Carefully, Milo climbed down the rope ladder and came face to face with Captain Whiskers and his crew of pirate kittens!

"Have you seen my favourite green crayon?" asked Milo,
as they bobbed over the waves searching for treasure.

But nobody had.

So Milo climbed into a rowing boat and headed for shore. He tied up his boat.

Then he followed the trail further,

and further,

and **further** until . . .

He was right in the middle of a desert.

Milo looked around but there wasn't a trace of
crayon in sight. He was all alone, well and truly lost.

With tears in his eyes, Milo looked up into the
night sky and there, to his amazement, was the trail!
Each sparkly star was connected like a giant join-the-dots
puzzle. "But I'll never get up there," sighed Milo, sadly.

"Don't be so sure about that!" said a voice.
Milo turned around and, out of nowhere,
a rocket had appeared.

"Come on, jump in!" called the pilot.
Milo couldn't believe his eyes.
He hurried inside and fastened his seat belt.

Suddenly, Milo was zooming through clouds
and space dust, past stars and planets,
all the way to . . .

The moon!

Milo bounced over moon rocks and around craters,
until he reached a moon cave.

And that was when he spotted the crayon trail culprit.
"What are you doing with MY favourite green crayon?"
asked Milo, "and who are you anyway?"

"I'm a Moon Kangaroo," replied the creature,
"and it's not your crayon, it's mine. I found it.
Come on, I'll show you."

The Moon Kangaroo took Milo to a
huge crater filled with toys.
"Every toy that gets lost on Earth ends
up here," she explained.
Milo had never seen so many toys before.
"Can we play with them?" he asked.

Milo and the Moon Kangaroo played for hours.

They doodled and coloured using Milo's crayons.

And they became the best of friends.

But, before long, it was time for Milo to go home.
"Can I have my green crayon back now?" he asked.
The Moon Kangaroo looked sad, and Milo felt mean
because he knew how much she liked to doodle.

Then he had an idea!

"You can have my pink crayon instead," he said.
The Moon Kangaroo bounced with happiness.
Pink was her favourite colour!

Sadly, Milo said goodbye to his new friend.

Then he followed the trail –

all the way home.

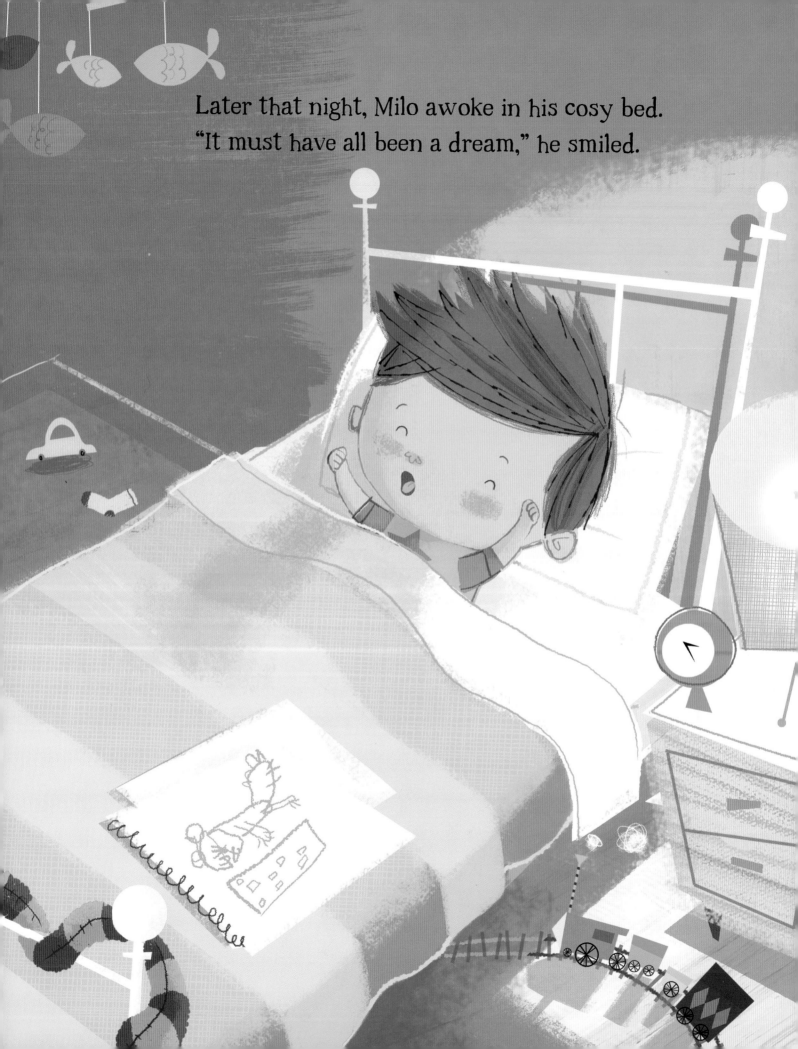

Later that night, Milo awoke in his cosy bed.
"It must have all been a dream," he smiled.

But when he looked inside his crayon box,
there was his green crayon ...

and an empty space
where the pink crayon should have been.

Could it **really** have been one big night-time adventure?

Thank you
Milo